IZZY
and the Candy Palace

by Isabel J.
Illustrations by J.H. Everett

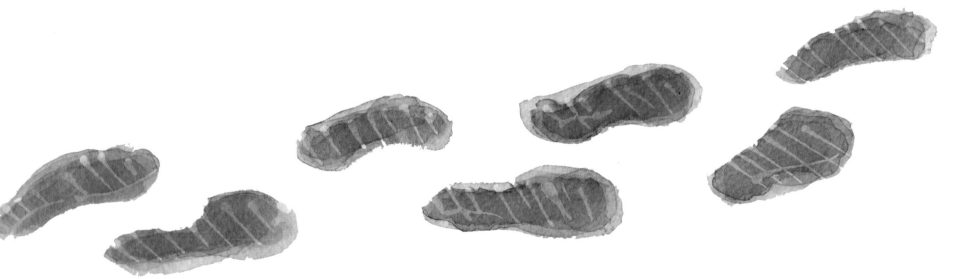

MMJ
Newport Beach • California

Yesterday I woke up to find a candy monster standing by my bed.

"Izzy, I have a gift for you,
because of the wonderful things you do!"

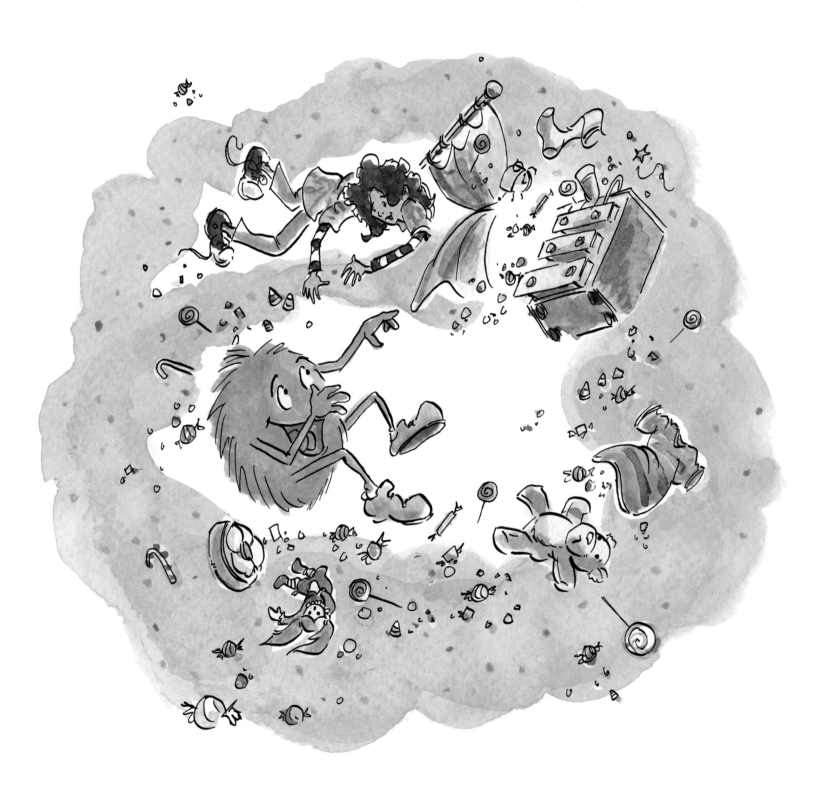

"You're such a kind and thoughtful girl,
I'll fill your room with chocolate swirl!"

I thought I was dreaming until
my brother and sister came in.
"Who's that?" asked Buddy.
"Never mind him. Look at all
this candy!" said Boo.

"Mom just left for the store, and I'm in charge,"
said Buddy.
"Then let's dig in!" I said.

"Izzy, I know you like to share,
so I'll make candy everywhere!"
said the monster,

as he danced

around the room.

"Yippee!"said Buddy.
"This is a dream come true!"

Candy in the dining room!

Candy in the living room!

Candy in the computer?

"STOP! Mister Monster, you're wrecking our house.
I'm no longer in charge. Izzy, this is your fault!" Buddy yelled.

"Holy Smackeroos!" I said. "Stop him before he goes outside!"

The candy monster ran toward the center of town,
right into the park.

Everybody was there for
Clean Up the Park Day.

"My gift to you is not complete, until there's candy in the street," said the monster.

People stared at us.

No one knew what to do, not even the mayor.
But Boo had an idea. She always does.

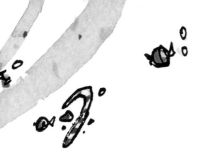

She grabbed a bullhorn and shouted, "Eat! Eat! Eat!"

All of the people in the park jumped onto the piles of candy and started eating.

But it didn't work. Not even a whole town could eat that much candy.
Then Mom called. "Hi, Honey. I'll be home soon.
You aren't making a mess, are you?"

"Izzy, I think you are tops!
    Have caramels and lemon drops!"
        the monster said as he kept going...

                and going...

                        and going...

Then the mayor had an idea.
He ordered the construction workers
to load the candy into their trucks
and haul it away.

"And somebody catch that MONSTER!"

But they couldn't. More candy appeared every time the monster waved his hands.

and MORE!

and more...

More...

I had to think of
SOMETHING.

"Isn't this fun?
Your friends are so clever!
I could make candy
in this town forever!"
said the monster.

The monster had given me an idea...
a really BIG idea.

"Come on," I said. "We've got to tell the mayor."

So I told the mayor
my big idea, and guess what?

He
loved
it!

The mayor told everybody, "Listen up!
This little girl has an idea that will work."

"Mister Monster," I said. "Please stop. We have enough candy.
Now come with me. I have a surprise you're going to like."

We loaded up the candy on dump trucks,
fire trucks, a helicopter, and a blimp.

We built a candy palace

in the middle of the park,

in the middle of our town...

for the candy monster,

and we asked him to stay.

Mom called again.
"I'm almost home,
but there's tons of traffic."

We had to get home
FAST!

We hopped into the police helicopter
and ZOOMED HOME!

There wasn't much time.

"Hurry! Mom's home," I said. "Shove everything in the closet!"

"Sorry it took me so long," Mom said. "I brought you lollipops."

"Uhhh... Thanks, Mom. Can we eat lunch first?"

"Thank you for your generous support of the Kids Cafe program."
~Isabel J.

100% of the profits from the sale of this book will be donated
by the MMJ Foundation to the Kids Cafe program of the
Second Harvest Food Bank of Orange County.

For more information, please visit www.thecandypalace.com

Text and illustration copyright ©2010 by The MMJ Foundation. • All rights reserved, including the right of reproduction in whole or in part in any form. • First edition 2010

Book design by Marilyn Scott-Waters and J.H. Everett • Additional poetry by Marilyn Scott-Waters
This book was typeset in Centaur. • The illustrations are rendered in watercolor and ink. • Printed in China

Library of Congress Control Number: 2010931337 • p. cm.

Summary: Izzy is befriended by a monster who fills her town with candy. • ISBN-13: 9780982797204 • ISBN-10: 0982797206 • 10 9 8 7 6 5 4 3 2 1

The MMJ Foundation • 4350 Von Karman, 4th Floor • Newport Beach, California 92660 • The MMJ Foundation is a 501(c)(3) non-profit corporation.